L.F.C.

THE OFFICIAL
LIVERPOOL FC
ANNUAL 2025

Designed by Adam Wilsher

A Grange Publication

© 2024. Published by Grange Communications Ltd., Edinburgh, under licence from The Liverpool Football Club. Printed in the EU.

ISBN 978-1-915879-88-2

CONTENTS

5   LFC HONOURS BOARD

6   WELCOME TO LIVERPOOL ARNE SLOT

10   LEAGUE CUP WINNERS 2024

15   THE LEAGUE CUP KINGS

16   ALISSON BECKER

17   TRENT ALEXANDER-ARNOLD

18   DANKE JÜRGEN

22   ANDY ROBERTSON

23   VIRGIL VAN DIJK

24   BORN IN THE USA: PRE-SEASON

26   GOAL OF THE SEASON

28   THE BIG LFC QUIZ

30   JOE GOMEZ

31   IBRAHIMA KONATÉ

32   KOP KIDS

34   ALI MAC'S COPA GLORY

35   SPOT THE DIFFERENCE

36   DOMINIK SZOBOSZLAI

37   ALEXIS MAC ALLISTER

38   HARVEY ELLIOTT: LIVING THE DREAM

40   WE'VE CONQUERED ALL OF EUROPE

42   CURTIS JONES

43   LUIS DÍAZ

44   LFC WOMEN

48   DARWIN NÚÑEZ

49   MOHAMED SALAH

50   EXPERIENCE THE MAGIC OF LFC

52   LFC CROSSWORD

53   WHO'S THE BOSS WORDSEARCH

54   CODY GAKPO

55   DIOGO JOTA

56   CIAO CHIESA!

58   LFC MEN'S TEAM

60   FIXTURE TRACKER

61   QUIZ & PUZZLE ANSWERS

62   SPOT THE PLAYERS

LFC HONOURS BOARD

19

LEAGUE TITLES
1900-01, 1905-06, 1921-22, 1922-23, 1946-47, 1963-64, 1965-66, 1972-73, 1975-76, 1976-77, 1978-79, 1979-80, 1981-82, 1982-83, 1983-84, 1985-86, 1987-88, 1989-90, 2019-20

6

EUROPEAN CUPS
1976-77, 1977-78, 1980-81, 1983-84, 2004-05, 2018-19

8

FA CUPS
1964-65, 1973-74, 1985-86, 1988-89, 1991-92, 2000-01, 2005-06, 2021-22

10

LEAGUE CUPS
1980-81, 1981-82, 1982-83, 1983-84, 1994-95, 2000-01, 2002-03, 2011-12, 2021-22, 2023-24

1

FIFA CLUB WORLD CUP
2019

2

WOMEN'S SUPER LEAGUE TITLES
2013, 2014

3

UEFA CUPS
1972-73, 1975-76, 2000-01

4

UEFA SUPER CUPS
1977, 2001, 2005, 2019

16 CHARITY / COMMUNITY SHIELDS 1964*, 1965*, 1966, 1974, 1976, 1977*, 1979, 1980, 1982, 1986*, 1988, 1989, 1990*, 2001, 2006, 2022 (*shared)

4 FA YOUTH CUPS
1996, 2006, 2007, 2019

4 DIVISION TWO
1893-94, 1895-96, 1904-05, 1961-62

1 FA WOMEN'S CHAMPIONSHIP
2021-22

1 LANCASHIRE LEAGUE
1892-93

18 RESERVE DIVISION ONE 1956-57, 1968-69, 1969-70, 1970-71, 1972-73, 1973-74, 1974-75, 1975-76, 1976-77, 1978-79, 1979-80, 1980-81, 1981-82, 1983-84, 1984-85, 1989-90, 1999-2000, 2007-08

1 FOOTBALL LEAGUE SUPER CUP
1986

Welcome to Liverpool
Arne Slot

With Arne Slot having replaced Jürgen Klopp at the Anfield helm during the summer of 2024, it's the dawn of a new era for Liverpool Football Club. Slot arrived from Feyenoord to accept the position of Head Coach and in doing so created history as the first Dutchman to take charge of the Reds. Let's find out a bit more about him...

Full Name:
Arend Martijn
(Arne) Slot
Place of Birth:
Bergentheim,
Netherlands
Date of Birth:
17 September 1978

Managerial Career

2016-2017: Cambuur
2019-2020: AZ Alkmaar
2021-2024: Feyenoord

Managerial Honours
Eredivisie 2022-23, KNVB
Cup 2023-24, Eredivisie
Manger of the Year
2021-22, 2022-23

Playing Career

Position:
Midfielder
1995-2002:
FC Zwolle
2002-2007:
NAC Breda
2007-2010:
Sparta
Rotterdam
2009-2010:
FC Zwolle
(loan)
2010-2013:
PEC Zwolle

Arne in his own words...

Leaving Feyenoord
"When I started there, the club was in quite a difficult place, didn't have a lot of money, ended up fifth I think. And we could change that around. Now, with two successive seasons of Champions League, winning the title once, winning the cup once, and the value the squad is completely different to three years ago – I think it's fair to say I left Feyenoord in a good place."

Liverpool being the right club for him
"I always knew that it had to be a fantastic club that I would leave Feyenoord for, and this was Liverpool and the league as well. I think it was a year ago that I was in the interest of a few Premier League clubs as well, but I decided to extend at Feyenoord with the idea of staying there two more seasons. But after a year, Liverpool came along and it wasn't a difficult choice to make. Although, like I said, I was really happy at Feyenoord, the way I work there with the fans, with the staff, with the players. But this was the possibility I had to take."

Speaking with Jürgen Klopp
"I think if someone worked at a club for nine years [and had] been so successful, you want to know all about it from him and you also want to know things of the players – although I think it is also important to get my own opinion about that. So, you can only use all this information he has because he did so well, not only in terms of results but I think also everybody saw in his farewell but also in the years before that how popular he was. He gave me more than a few good tips but I think what stood out for me was that he was so happy for me and that – and I think he said this in the media as well – he would be my biggest fan from now on because he supports Liverpool in the best possible way, and you don't see this very often. So, it says a lot about his character, the way he handled this situation as well."

The dawn of a new Anfield era

"Of course, there is change but a lot of things are still the same as well. I think the players are still the same, which is probably the most important thing because, of course, we as managers sometimes tend to think that we have a lot of influence, which we can have, but in the end it comes down to the players. And I think the fans are still the same, so many things are still the same and yeah, we are going to try to work on what Jürgen left behind and we will see a lot of similar things. But, of course, I bring my own things to the table as well and I think that's also what is expected of me."

The role of 'head coach'

"For me, it is normal because this is the way it is in Europe and in Holland. I don't think there is much of a change between a head coach and a manager, it's just that by being a head coach I can go in fully to the things I would like to do. So, work with the team, prepare the team in the best possible way, and me and Richard [Hughes] are going to work together when it comes to transfers but not only the two of us – there is a big backroom staff included in this as well. I think for me it is the way I have worked always and it for me is the ideal way of working."

His coaching style

"I will be really focused on the training ground. I think there is the place where you can influence the most and you have to influence the most, because you have to influence your players, common to [the] game model and your game plan. And I think that's where it's all about – to find a way of playing which suits the players the best and then adjust maybe with the game plan a bit where we can win a few things. But that's all tactical and I think there's something else towards being a head coach or a manager or the way

you want to call it and that is the relations you have with people. The relationships I have with my staff but also the players, how they get along with each other and the relationships between staff and players We have to find a way that people get used to me and used to the new staff that's coming in, and get the same energy in this building and eventually into the stadium as well because that's where it's all about – we have to perform during the games. But to perform there, I think it's important to have a good idea of how we want to play and a good energy within the team and within the people who are working at Liverpool."

The Liverpool he inherited

"[A] real good team, real good players, managed to be on top for a very long time, but I think in the end we would all love to see Liverpool a bit higher than third place and this is the challenge we are facing now – to build on from what we have. I have all the confidence in this because of the players, that we can add a few things where we hopefully can get a bit more points than 82, which is necessary with the likes of Arsenal and City, to end up hopefully a bit higher than we did this season."

Similarities between Liverpool and former club Feyenoord

"Both are cities alongside the river, people work on the docks, it's a hard working class, fans that appreciate seeing the team. I think these clubs like Feyenoord and Liverpool, from what I saw of it, it just means a bit more for the fans, it just means a bit more if the team does well than at some other

places around the world. This is what I felt at Feyenoord and I'm expecting to feel the same here at Anfield as well."

Message for the fans

"There is a change but the change hopefully isn't that big, because we still have the same players, we still have the same fans – and if the both of them are going to do the same job, that will make my life a lot more easy! I'm expecting them to show up again in the upcoming season, and the same for the players. I will do everything within my interest and power to lead the team in the best possible way."

The managerial footsteps Arne follows in at Anfield

1892-1895: **William Barclay**
1895-1896: **John McKenna**
1896-1915: **Tom Watson**
1919-1922: **Dave Ashworth**
1923-1928: **Matt McQueen**
1928-1936: **George Patterson**
1936-1951: **George Kay**
1951-1956: **Don Welsh**
1956-1959: **Phil Taylor**
1959-1974: **Bill Shankly**
1974-1983: **Bob Paisley**
1983-1985: **Joe Fagan**
1985-1991: **Kenny Dalglish**
1991-1994: **Graeme Souness**
1994-1998: **Roy Evans**
1998: **Roy Evans/Gerard Houllier**
1998-2004: **Gerard Houllier**
2004-2010: **Rafael Benítez**
2010-2011: **Roy Hodgson**
2011-2012: **Kenny Dalglish**
2012-2015: **Brendan Rodgers**
2015-2024: **Jürgen Klopp**

THE PERFECT TEN
LEAGUE 🏆 CUP
WINNERS 2024!

Liverpool's Road to Wembley...

3rd Round
Leicester City (h) 3-1
Scorers: **Gakpo, Szoboszlai, Jota**

Team: Kelleher, Konaté, Tsimikas (Chambers), Quansah, Endō, Jones (Bajčetić), Elliott, Gravenberch (Szoboszlai), Gakpo, Jota, Doak (Núñez).

Liverpool's quest for League Cup success got off to the worst possible start when Championship side Leicester took the lead in front of the Kop after just three minutes. Despite hitting the woodwork twice and creating numerous chances, it wasn't until the second half that goals from Cody Gakpo, Dominik Szoboszlai and Diogo Jota ensured there would be no shock result.

4th Round
Bournemouth (a) 2-1
Scorers: **Gakpo, Núñez**

Team: Kelleher, Gomez, Tsimikas, Matip, Quansah, Endō (Alexander-Arnold), Szoboszlai (Gravenberch), Jones (Mac Allister), Elliott (Núñez), Salah, Gakpo (Jota).

A stunning strike by Darwin Núñez clinched victory for Liverpool in this all-Premier League tie on the south coast. Cody Gakpo had earlier opened the scoring only for Bournemouth to level in the second half. Six minutes later Núñez cut in from the left to unleash an unstoppable curling shot into the top right corner and it was enough to secure a quarter-final berth.

5th Round
West Ham United (h) 5-1
Scorers: Szoboszlai, Jones (2), Gakpo, Salah

Team: Kelleher, Gomez, Van Dijk (Konaté), Tsimikas (Bradley), Quansah, Endō (Alexander-Arnold), Szoboszlai (Salah), Jones, Elliott, Núñez, Gakpo (Díaz).

Five days before Christmas, Liverpool turned on the style against West Ham at Anfield to emphatically book their place in the last four of the competition. Dominik Szoboszlai broke the deadlock just before the half hour mark before further goals after the break from Curtis Jones (2), Cody Gakpo and Mo Salah completed the rout.

Semi-Final 1st Leg
Fulham (h) 2-1
Scorers: **Jones, Gakpo**

Team: Kelleher, Gomez, Van Dijk, Konaté, Bradley, Mac Allister, Jones, Elliott (Gakpo), Gravenberch (Núñez), Díaz, Jota.

Fulham shocked the Kop with an impressive start and deservedly took the lead before a second half comeback saw the tie swing back in Liverpool's favour, courtesy of two goals in three minutes from Cody Gakpo and Curtis Jones. The advantage remained a slender one though, meaning there was still everything to play for in London the following week.

Semi-Final 2nd Leg
Fulham (a) 1-1
Scorer: **Díaz**

Team: Kelleher, Gomez, Van Dijk, Quansah, Bradley, Mac Allister (Jones), Elliott, Gravenberch (Clark), Díaz, Núñez (Jota), Gakpo (Konaté).

An early goal by Luis Díaz gave Liverpool breathing space in the tie and put them within touching distance of the final but, after Fulham hit back in the second half, a nervous finale ensued before supporters could start making plans for another trip to Wembley.

Final
Wembley Stadium
Sunday 25 February 2024
Attendance: 88,888

Chelsea 1-0

Scorer: **Van Dijk** (118)

Liverpool: Kelleher, Van Dijk, Konaté (Quansah), Robertson (Tsimikas), Bradley (Clark), Endō, Mac Allister (McConnell), Elliott, Gravenberch (Gomez), Díaz, Gakpo (Danns).

Chelsea: Petrović, Gusto, Disasi, Colwill, Chilwell (Chalobah), Fernandez, Caicedo, Palmer, Gallagher (Madueke), Sterling (Nkunku), Jackson (Mudryk).

Liverpool disproved the theory that you 'win nothing with kids' to claim a record extending 10th League Cup on an eventful and unforgettable afternoon at Wembley. Just like in 2022, it was Chelsea who provided the opposition and another tense, nail-biting encounter ensued. Jürgen Klopp's injury-stricken squad featured several inexperienced youngsters and, as the drama unfolded, the odds became increasingly stacked against them. VAR, the woodwork and impressive goalkeeping all contrived to deny both sides and it wasn't until near the end of extra-time, with a penalty shoot-out seemingly imminent that Virgil van Dijk eventually broke the deadlock. Kostas Tsimikas swung in a corner from the right and the Reds' captain headed home the winner at the end of the stadium where the majority of Liverpool fans were housed. Klopp's team had overcome adversity once more and the three-handled trophy was on its way back to Anfield yet again, sparking wild celebrations on and off the pitch.

"What happened here was absolutely insane, these things are not possible. The team, a squad, an academy full of character. I am so proud I could be part of that tonight. The craziest thing is we deserved it. We had lucky moments, they had lucky moments. The boys showed up, it was really cool." Jürgen Klopp

"It was a very tough match and big matches are played this way. We have a year with lots of matches, prepare like that for every game, we knew it would be a challenge but we prepared really well." Luís Díaz

"These are the moments you dream about. It's better for the heart than penalties! Another amazing moment for me, I'm delighted." Caoimhín Kelleher

"It's incredible. We got the job done. I'm so proud of the team. They all played their part. An intense game for both sides, they had chances, we had chances and [it's] amazing. First trophy as the Liverpool captain – it's all for the fans so let's enjoy it. You should always savour the good moments and this is definitely one of them. We will never take these things for granted, we are very, very blessed." Virgil van Dijk

A total of 27 players contributed during the course of Liverpool's victorious 2023/24 League Cup winning campaign.

	Appearances	Goals
Caoimhín Kelleher	6	0
Joel Matip	1	0
Conor Bradley	4	0
Luke Chambers	1	0
Jarell Quansah	5	0
Joe Gomez	5	0
Ibrahima Konaté	5	0
Virgil van Dijk	4	1
Trent Alexander-Arnold	2	0
Andy Robertson	1	0
Kostas Tsimikas	4	0
Wataru Endō	4	0
Curtis Jones	5	3
Harvey Elliott	6	0

	Appearances	Goals
Dominik Szoboszlai	3	2
Ryan Gravenberch	5	0
Alexis Mac Allister	4	0
Stefan Bajčetić	1	0
Bobby Clark	2	0
James McConnell	1	0
Mohamed Salah	2	1
Diogo Jota	4	1
Cody Gakpo	6	4
Ben Doak	1	0
Jayden Danns	1	0
Darwin Núñez	5	1
Luis Díaz	4	1

The League Cup Kings

No club has won the League Cup more times than Liverpool.

Number of wins

10	**LIVERPOOL**
8	Manchester City
6	Manchester United
5	Chelsea, Aston Villa
4	Tottenham Hotspur
3	Nottingham Forest
2	Arsenal, Norwich City, Birmingham City, Wolverhampton Wanderers
1	West Bromwich Albion, Middlesbrough, Queens Park Rangers, Leeds United, Stoke City, Luton Town, Sheffield Wednesday, Swindon Town, Oxford United, Blackburn Rovers, Swansea City

Liverpool's 10 League Cup triumphs

1. 1981 v West Ham United 2-1 (Villa Park)
2. 1982 v Tottenham Hotspur 3-1 (Wembley)
3. 1983 v Manchester United 2-1 (Wembley)
4. 1984 v Everton 1-0 (Maine Road)
5. 1995 v Bolton Wanderers 2-1 (Wembley)
6. 2001 v Birmingham City 1-1* (Millenium Stadium)
7. 2003 v Manchester United 2-0 (Millenium Stadium)
8. 2012 v Cardiff City 2-2* (Wembley)
9. 2022 v Chelsea 0-0* (Wembley)
10. 2024 v Chelsea 1-0 (Wembley)

* Won on pens

CARABAO CUP FINAL 2024 WINNERS

L.F.C.

ALISSON BECKER

1

NATIONALITY:
Brazilian

DATE OF BIRTH:
2 October 1992

GAMES: 263

GOALS: 1

ASSISTS: 3

HONOURS:
FA Cup (2022), League Cup
(2022, 2024), Premier League
(2019-20), Champions
League (2019), FIFA Club
World Cup (2019)

L.F.C.

TRENT ALEXANDER-ARNOLD

66

NATIONALITY:
English

DATE OF BIRTH:
7 October 1998

GAMES: 310

GOALS: 19

ASSISTS: 79

HONOURS:
FA Community Shield (2022),
FA Cup (2022), League Cup
(2022, 2024), Premier League
(2019-20), Champions
League (2019), UEFA Super
Cup (2019), FIFA Club World
Cup (2019)

Danke Jürgen

He turned doubters into believers and underachievers into winners... Jürgen Klopp's managerial tenure at Liverpool will forever be remembered as one of the greatest periods in the club's history.

Eight trophies in just under nine years and a multitude of unforgettable moments along the way, it was an emotional rollercoaster of a journey that swept through Anfield, England, Europe and the world.

Not since the days of Bill Shankly had Liverpool supporters felt a connection to their manager like they did with this man and so it was with a heavy heart, and plenty of tears, that they bid a reluctant but fond farewell to him in May 2024.

Four months earlier, Klopp announced he would be stepping down as manager of the Reds and to say it came as a shock would be a massive understatement. As the news reverberated across the planet, it stunned everyone to the core and left them scratching their heads in bewilderment.

For many Liverpudlians, the guy from the Black Forest in Germany had given them the best footballing moments of their lives and they hoped he would have continued in the job for the foreseeable future.

Since taking over from Brendan Rodgers in October 2015, Klopp had completely transformed the club, reinvigorated the fanbase and brought the good times back.

A sixth European crown was secured in Madrid 2019, a first-ever world title followed later that same year and then, in 2020, he delivered what all at Liverpool had craved for 30 years when putting the Liver Bird back on its perch as Champions of England.

Further success came in the domestic cup competitions and the team became perennial title challengers. With a bit more luck the trophy haul could have been even greater.

So many of the 'mentality monster' players Klopp brought to the club and those whose talents he nurtured are now considered to be among the best to have pulled on a red shirt, while the teams he »

assembled, with their 'heavy metal' football, are rightly compared to the famous Liverpool sides of the sixties, seventies and eighties.

Aside from all the success and silverware though, this adopted Scouser was loved by the supporters for just being himself; how he acted, the things he said, the passion he showed and the fact he was fully in tune with his people.

After fittingly signing off as Liverpool manager with a 2-0 win over Wolves on the final day of the of the 2023/24 season, Klopp paid tribute to the crowd that had given him nothing but their full backing and reassured them that the club's future remains safe in the hands of Arne Slot, the man he would be passing the baton on to.

"You welcome the new manager like you welcomed me. You go all-in from the first day. And when it's hard you keep believing and you push the team," urged the departing boss. "Change is good. It doesn't feel like an end, it just feels like the start. I saw a football team today full of talent, youth, creativity, desire and greed. That's one part of development, that's what you need.

"This club is in a better moment than ever, maybe not ever, I'd have to ask Kenny [Dalglish], but since a long time! We have this wonderful stadium, this wonderful training centre, we have you. The superpower of world football, wow. Since today I'm one of you and I keep believing in you. I stay a believer, 100 percent. I love you to bits. On my jumper is 'Thank you Luv' and 'I will never walk alone again'. Thank you for that! You are the best people in the world. Thank you!"

Before walking off the Anfield pitch for a final time, Klopp chanted loudly in a show of support for his successor. It was a true measure of the man he is. Although he once famously described himself as the 'Normal One', there was nothing normal about his nine seasons at the Liverpool helm. Jürgen Klopp's time in charge was beyond special and will never be forgotten. Thanks for the memories...

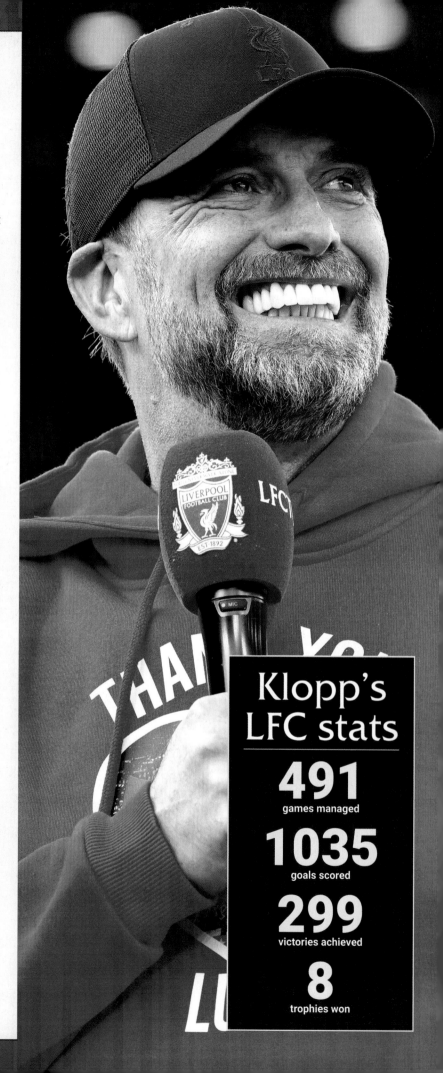

Klopp's LFC stats

491
games managed

1035
goals scored

299
victories achieved

8
trophies won

KLOPP'S LFC TROPHY-WINNING TIMELINE

JUNE 2019
CHAMPIONS LEAGUE

AUGUST 2019
UEFA SUPER CUP

DECEMBER 2019
FIFA CLUB WORLD CUP

JUNE 2020
FA PREMIER LEAGUE

FEBRUARY 2022
LEAGUE CUP

MAY 2022
FA CUP

AUGUST 2022
FA COMMUNITY SHIELD

FEBRUARY 2024
LEAGUE CUP

*Klopp was also twice named Manager of the Year and awarded the Freedom of the City of Liverpool

L.F.C.

ANDY ROBERTSON

26

NATIONALITY:
Scottish

DATE OF BIRTH:
11 March 1994

GAMES: 297

GOALS: 11

ASSISTS: 65

HONOURS:
FA Community Shield (2022),
FA Cup (2022), League Cup
(2022, 2024), Premier League
(2019-20), Champions
League (2019), UEFA Super
Cup (2019), FIFA Club World
Cup (2019)

L.F.C.

VIRGIL VAN DIJK

4

NATIONALITY:
Dutch

DATE OF BIRTH:
8 July 1991

GAMES: 270

GOALS: 23

ASSISTS: 9

HONOURS:
FA Community Shield (2022),
FA Cup (2022), League Cup
(2022, 2024), Premier League
(2019-20), Champions
League (2019), UEFA Super
Cup (2019), FIFA Club World
Cup (2019)

Born In The USA

Liverpool warmed up for the 2024/25 season with a successful summer tour of America.

Despite being without several key players, all eyes were focussed on how the new-look Reds would fare and they did not disappoint.

During a 12-day stay in the States, a brand new era was ushered in as Arne Slot's team blazed a trail through Pittsburgh, Philadelphia and South Carolina.

Packed-out stadiums greeted them at each venue and provided a fitting backdrop to three impressive victories as lasting memories were made for the club's ever-increasing US fanbase.

WILLIAMS-BRICE STADIUM

UNITED vs LIVERPOOL FC

WILLIAMS-BRICE STADIUM AUG 3

THE COCKPIT

26 July
Acrisure Stadium, Pittsburgh
Liverpool 1 v 0 Real Betis
Goalscorer: Dominik Szoboszlai
Attendance: 42,679

31 July
Lincoln Financial Field, Philadelphia
Liverpool 2 v 1 Arsenal
Goalscorers: Mohamed Salah, Fábio Carvalho
Attendance: 69,879

4 August
Williams-Brice Stadium, South Carolina
Liverpool 3 v 0 Manchester United
Goalscorers: Fábio Carvalho, Curtis Jones, Kostas Tsimikas
Attendance: 77,559

GOAL OF THE SEASON

A countdown of the ten best Liverpool goals scored during the 2023/24 campaign.

10

Conor Bradley
v Chelsea
(h) Premier League,
31 January 2024

9

Darwin Núñez
v Brentford
(a) Premier League,
17 February 2024

8

Mohamed Salah
v Brighton & Hove
Albion
(h) Premier League,
31 March 2024

7

Dominik Szoboszlai
v Leicester City
(h) League Cup 3rd round,
27 September 2023

6

Trent Alexander-Arnold
v Manchester City
(a) Premier League,
25 November 2023

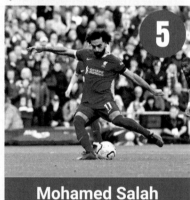

5

Mohamed Salah
v Everton
(h) Premier League,
21 October 2023

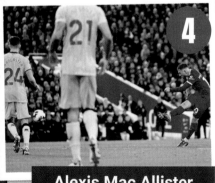

4

Alexis Mac Allister
v Sheffield United
(h) Premier League,
4 April 2024

3

Darwin Núñez
v Newcastle United
(a) Premier League,
27 August 2023

2

Harvey Elliott
v Tottenham Hotspur
(h) Premier League,
5 May 2024

1

Alexis Mac Allister
v Fulham
(h) Premier League,
3 December 2023

Goal Stats 2023/24

TOTAL NUMBER OF LIVERPOOL GOALS SCORED

142

AVERAGE GOALS PER GAME

2.90

WHEN THE GOALS WERE SCORED

1 to 15 minutes
12

16 to 30 minutes
18

31 to 45 minutes
25

46 to 60 minutes
23

61 to 75 minutes
22

76 to 90 minutes
40

91 to 120 minutes
2

BREAKDOWN OF GOALS SCORED PER COMPETITION

Premier League
86

Europa League
29

League Cup
14

FA Cup
13

THE BIG ⭐ LIVERPOOL FC QUIZ

GENERAL KNOWLEDGE

1. Who scored the last goal of Jürgen Klopp's reign as Liverpool manager?

2. What club did Arne Slot lead to league and cup success in Holland?

3. Against which team did Mo Salah score his first competitive Liverpool goal?

4. Who did Virgil van Dijk succeed as Liverpool captain?

5. Which team were beaten 9-0 at Anfield in August 2022?

6. Conor Bradley plays international football for which country?

7. At which stadium did goalkeeper Alisson Becker score for Liverpool in 2021?

8. Which current player made his debut as a 16 year old in 2019?

9. In what month were Liverpool confirmed as Premier League Champions in 2020?

10. Who was the only player to score in both halves of Liverpool's 7-0 win over Manchester United in 2023?

11. In which competition did Jayden Danns score his first senior Liverpool goal?

12. Which team did Liverpool play twice at Wembley in 2022?

13. Who scored the winning goal when Liverpool won the FIFA Club World Cup in 2019?

14. How many times have Liverpool FC Women won the WSL?

15. In which country did Jürgen Klopp win his first trophy as Liverpool manager?

RETRO REDS

1. From which club did Liverpool sign Luis Suárez?

2. Who is Liverpool's all-time record appearance holder?

3. How many times have Liverpool won the UEFA Super Cup?

4. Name the manager who guided Liverpool to a cup treble in 2001?

5. Which Liverpool striker won the European Golden Boot award in 1984?

WHICH LIVERPOOL PLAYER AM I?

1. I was signed from Bayern Munich in 2023.

2. I played for Uruguay in the 2024 Copa America.

3. I am currently Liverpool's longest-serving player.

4. I lifted the League Cup as captain at Wembley in 2024.

5. I scored the fastest hat-trick in Champions League history.

MISSING MEN

Can you spot which two players are missing from this Liverpool line-up?

UP FOR THE CUP

In which year did Liverpool win the following trophies for the first time?

| FA Cup | European Cup/ Champions League | UEFA Cup/ Europa League | League Cup | FIFA Club World Cup |

TRANSFER WINDOW

Can you identify these Liverpool players from three of the former clubs they've played for?

#			
1.	QUEENS PARK	DUNDEE UNITED	HULL CITY
2.	BASEL	CHELSEA	ROMA
3.	ARGENTINOS JUNIORS	BOCA JUNIORS	BRIGHTON & HOVE ALBION
4.	ATLÉTICO MADRID	PORTO	WOLVERHAMPTON WANDERERS
5.	URAWA RED DIAMONDS	SINT-TRUIDEN	STUTTGART

Answers page 61

L.F.C.

JOE GOMEZ

2

NATIONALITY:
English

DATE OF BIRTH:
23 May 1997

GAMES: 224

GOALS: 0

ASSISTS: 9

Honours:
FA Community Shield (2022),
FA Cup (2022), League Cup
(2022, 2024), Premier League
(2019-20), Champions
League (2019), UEFA Super
Cup (2019), FIFA Club World
Cup (2019)

L.F.C.

IBRAHIMA KONATÉ

5

NATIONALITY:
French

DATE OF BIRTH:
25 May 1999

GAMES: 90

GOALS: 3

ASSISTS: 2

HONOURS:
FA Community Shield (2022),
FA Cup (2022), League Cup
(2022, 2024)

31

KOP KIDS

Four Liverpool starlets sit down to discuss their meteoric rise through the ranks and reflect on some key personal moments from a 2023/24 season that none of them will ever forget.

JARELL QUANSAH
Debut:
27 August 2023 v Newcastle United (a)

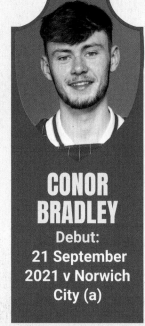

CONOR BRADLEY
Debut:
21 September 2021 v Norwich City (a)

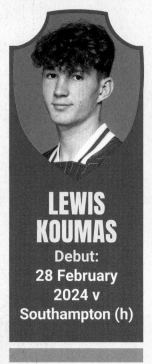

LEWIS KOUMAS
Debut:
28 February 2024 v Southampton (h)

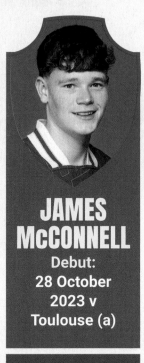

JAMES McCONNELL
Debut:
28 October 2023 v Toulouse (a)

What's been that realisation moment, where you couldn't quite believe what was happening to you?

CB: It was probably after the Chelsea league game [when I scored], it was just the game of my life, I don't think... I could do no wrong that night. All my friends were over at my house with me that night, and I just remember saying, "What has just happened?" Like, it was crazy. And, yeah, that was probably the moment for me.

LK: The night of the Southampton game, and also the Final... It's all been mad.

At the start of last season, how likely was this scenario that you'd all be sat here now talking about first team debuts, first goals for Liverpool, etc?

JM: Back then I was probably just happy training with them and waiting to get the text every night to see if I was back with the U21s or first team. So, yeah, it's definitely quite surreal.

JQ: It's been a whirlwind, really. Just getting to play with probably, of this generation, the best centre-back [van Dijk] that there's been. It just gives me time and opportunity to learn off him, really.

That Newcastle game was crazy...

JQ: Yeah, that's one of them you can't put into words, for that to be

my debut. Yeah, it's polar opposite to what it was a season before, to be fair.

What are the nerves like at that precise moment?

JQ: It is pressure, but in my head there's no reason for me to feel that pressure in that moment. I think the manager's trusted me, he's watched me play. For everyone else, it's: "What's going on?", but for him, he's seen me play for a couple of years and actually hit the ground running in pre-season. So, I think for him to think I'm good enough for that level, then to come on and hold my own really was a good moment.

Who, out of you all, has been the most equipped to walk into that dressing room and looked most at home off the pitch?

JM: Conor and Jarell have been around it a little bit longer, so I'll give it to them, easy option.

JQ: Yeah, I think we've been around

the changing room a little bit now, and I think you have to build these relationships, and we're part of the team now. So having everyone be able to show their personality and add to the team is necessary really.

Who's been great with you then, senior-player wise?

LK: All of them. All of them are very welcoming and speak to you, you can get on with them, which is good.

JM: Yeah, really welcoming. They don't just talk to us, they actually have a laugh and take the mick a bit and stuff like that to make us feel comfortable. In particular, Curt [Jones] I think has really helped the link between the two changing rooms, but yeah, they've all been really good and credit to all them.

You've got this special friendship together now, so the fact that you've done this, you've achieved this together, how special has that been?

CB: I only moved over officially when I was 16, but I'd been coming over on trial since I was about 11, 12. So I've been with Jarell for eight years, nearly 10 years maybe. And, yeah, to see him come on at St. James' Park and do what he did was special.

JQ: Having that game against Chelsea... I wish you could get the pictures from that game of me on the bench, literally I couldn't stop smiling. The stuff he [Conor] was doing... One of them games where everything goes well for you, and I was just so happy for him.

Let's talk a little bit about another youngster who broke though, Jayden Danns. Is he a true finisher then?

LK: Yeah, 100 percent, if there's a goal to be scored, he'll score it.

CB: I know he's a good finisher from what I've seen in training, but to do what he did [against Southampton], just dinking it over the keeper, was special. And even the second one, he was on his toes just to go and bury it.

LK: Yeah, I had no doubt. He's an unreal finisher and I was just absolutely buzzing when he hit the back of the net.

JM: He's got that natural instinct in front of goal to sniff out a chance. And I think you see that with his second one, he's anticipated Con having a shot when no-one else has! And he's finished it, he's finished it really nicely. So I'm buzzing for him.

Have you thought about what this perhaps does for the Academy? All of the things that you lads have achieved gives so much hope to the next generation coming through...

JM: I think it's been happening ever since Jürgen Klopp came in, the likes of Trent, Curt, and rightfully so it gives them confidence and belief to keep working hard in the under-16s or the under-18s. Because ultimately they could end up winning something like we did. So you've just got to be ready to take your chance.

How comfortable are you with that now, that there's kids looking up to you and saying, "What an example this young lad has set for us"?

LK: Yeah, it feels weird, to hear that, to be honest. It wasn't long ago that I was doing it with some of those lads. I hope the Academy gets the credit it deserves because it's helped and prepared us really well.

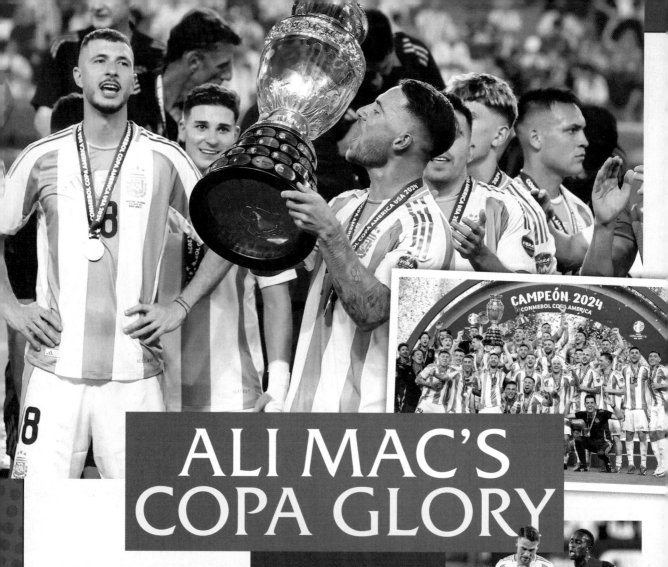

ALI MAC'S COPA GLORY

Alexis Mac Allister became a double international Champion during the summer of 2024 as Argentina lifted the Copa America title.

A World Cup winner in 2022, Mac Allister once again played an integral role in his country's success during the month-long tournament hosted by the United States.

The Liverpool midfielder featured in all but one of *La Albiceleste's* six games and scored a penalty in the quarter-final shoot-out victory over Ecuador.

In the final against Columbia, he came face to face with Anfield team-mate Luis Díaz and Argentina eventually prevailed, winning 1-0 after extra-time.

Mac Allister became the fourth Liverpool player to win the Copa America.

MACCA'S MAP TO COPA AMERICA GLORY

Group stage
Argentina 2-0 Canada
(played full game)
Argentina 1-0 Chile
(played full game)
Argentina 2-0 Peru
(unused substitute)

Quarter-final
Argentina 1-1 Ecuador
(played full game)
*won 4-2 on penalties

Semi-final
Argentina 2-0 Canada
(played 78 minutes)

Final
Argentina 1-0 Colombia
(played 97 minutes)

LIVERPOOL'S PREVIOUS CONMEBOL CHAMPIONS:
2011 – Luis Suárez (Uruguay) 2019 – Alisson Becker & Roberto Firmino (Brazil)

SPOT THE DIFFERENCE

Can you spot the ten differences between these two pictures from Liverpool's visit to Ipswich Town?

Answers page 61

DOMINIK SZOBOSZLAI

8

NATIONALITY:
Hungarian

DATE OF BIRTH:
25 October 2000

GAMES: 45

GOALS: 7

ASSISTS: 4

HONOURS:
League Cup (2024)

L.F.C.

ALEXIS MAC ALLISTER

10

MIDFIELDER

NATIONALITY:
Argentinian

DATE OF BIRTH:
24 December 1998

GAMES: 46

GOALS: 7

ASSISTS: 7

HONOURS:
League Cup (2024)

37

HARVEY ELLIOTT
LIVING THE DREAM

Despite his tender age, Harvey Elliott is already considered to be a regular and important member of Liverpool's first team squad.

The 21-year old was just 16 when he joined the club from Fulham in 2019 and is well on his way to fulfilling the early promise he showed at Craven Cottage.

A gifted attacking midfielder, Elliott has since amassed over a century of first team appearances for the Reds, while helping them to domestic league and cup success in the process.

He's also represented England at under-21 level and is hoping his career at Anfield, with the team he supported as a boy, will be a long and fruitful one.

How do you reflect on your time at the club so far?
"It's gone very quick! It's been five unbelievable years and hopefully many more to come. I just need to stay working hard and keep getting my head down and playing for this team and playing for the badge. I've loved every minute of it."

How have you found the transition from working under former manager Jürgen Klopp to new head coach Arne Slot?
"You're always learning, you're always having to adapt and to be a better player, be a better person. It's one of those situations now [where] we just need to keep on going and keep listening to the staff and the boss, and make sure we apply it into the games and into the training sessions. I'm sure we'll be fine. It's more about in possession now and the players are really excited. There's certain patterns and the way we play, it's got a good buzz around the team.

How do the new tactics suit your own style of play?

"I think the positions [in the] formations that he plays, there's a few that are very my style of play, especially the No.10 role. I play it at England [U21s], so I know it very, very well. I feel like it's my most comfortable position, especially where I can receive it, how to receive it. It's kind of the bread and butter for me and I know it to a tee."

Would you say that is now your preferred position?

"I hope so, yeah. It's something I'm working towards. I need to prove it – it's not really going to be given to me, especially with the quality that we have in and around the team. It's going to be very hard. I'll be happy to play wherever but if I had to choose a specific position, it would be there."

What are your personal aspirations for the 2024/25 season?

"I want to play more games this season, I want to start more [and] kind of cement my spot in the team. I'll do what it takes. I feel like I'm at the age now where I need to take a lot of responsibility on. It's upon myself now to go out and do it. This season is going to be a big one for me. I just need to keep working hard and keep taking on the responsibility myself and just apply it into everything that I do."

And from a team perspective?

"I think we can achieve everything. It's just down to us as players to go and prove it and make sure we do it. We have the team, we have the backing from everyone and, most importantly, we have the fans. Wherever we go, they're travelling in numbers and always supporting us. I feel like as a club we can achieve great things again and we just need to keep pushing for it."

HARVEY'S MILESTONE LFC MOMENTS

28 July 2019 – signs for Liverpool from Fulham

25 September 2019 – first team debut v MK Dons (a) League Cup 3rd round

2 January 2020 – Premier League debut v Sheffield United (h)

6 February 2022 – first senior goal v Cardiff City (h) FA Cup 4th round

16 February 2022 – Champions League debut v Inter Milan (a)

27 February 2022 – came on as subsitute in League Cup Final victory v Chelsea at Wembley

28 May 2022 – unused subsitute in Champions League Final v Real Madrid in Paris

27 August 2022 – first Premier League goal v Bournemouth (h)

12 October 2022 – first Champions League goal v Rangers (a)

25 February 2024 – plays all 120 minutes of League Cup Final victory v Chelsea at Wembley

HARVEY'S SEASON-BY-SEASON LFC STATS

Season	Games	Goals
2019/20	8	0
2020/21*	1	0
2021/22	11	1
2022/23	46	5
2023/24	53	4

*(majority of season spent on loan at Blackburn Rovers)

"WE'VE CONQUERED ALL OF EUROPE"

Celebrating 60 years of Liverpool FC's participation in European competition

REDS IN EUROPE

Played:
441

Won:
247

Drawn:
95

Lost:
99

Goals Scored:
808

Goals Conceded:
390

THE TROPHIES

6

European Cup/UEFA Champions League
1977	Borussia Mönchengladbach 3-1
1978	Club Brugge 1-0
1981	Real Madrid 1-0
1984	AS Roma 1-1 (4-2 on pens)
2005	AC Milan 3-3 (3-2 on pens)
2019	Tottenham Hotspur 2-0

3

UEFA Cup
1973	Borussia Mönchengladbach 3-2 (on aggregate)
1976	Club Brugge 4-3 (on aggregate)
2001	Alavés 5-4

4

UEFA Super Cup
1977	SV Hamburg 7-1 (on aggregate)
2001	Bayern Munich 3-2
2005	CSKA Moscow 3-1
2019	Cheslea 2-2 (5-4 on pens)

FIRST GAME

5-0 v KR Reykjavik (a) 17 August 1964, European Cup preliminary round 1st leg

Team: Tommy Lawrence, Gerry Byrne, Ronnie Moran, Gordon Milne, Ron Yeats, Willie Stevenson, Ian Callaghan, Roger Hunt, Phil Chisnall, Gordon Wallace, Peter Thompson
Scorers: Wallace (2), Hunt (2), Chisnall

MOST EUROPEAN APPEARANCES

1 Jamie Carragher – 150
2 Steven Gerrard – 130
3 Sami Hyypiä – 94
4 Ian Callaghan – 89
5 Tommy Smith – 85

TOP EUROPEAN GOALSCORERS

1 Mohamed Salah – 47
2 Steven Gerrard – 41
3 Sadio Mané – 26
4 Roberto Firmino – 24
5 Michael Owen – 22

MOST VISITED COUNTRIES

Spain – 25
Germany, Italy – 21
France – 20
Portugal – 14
Belgium, Netherlands – 10
Scotland – 9
Russia, Switzerland, Turkey – 8
Hungary, Romania – 7
Finland – 6
Austria, Bulgaria, Greece – 5

MOST FREQUENT OPPONENTS

Benfica – 12
Chelsea, Real Madrid – 11
Barcelona, Porto – 10
Bayern Munich – 9
Atletico Madrid, Napoli – 8
AS Roma – 7

FIVE FAMOUS ANFIELD EUROPEAN NIGHTS

Inter Milan, European Cup semi-final 1st leg, 4 May 1965, won 3-1
Saint-Étienne, European Cup quarter-final 2nd leg, 16 March 1977, won 3-1
Chelsea, Champions League semi-final 2nd leg, 3 May 2005, won 1-0
Real Madrid, Champions League round of 16 2nd leg, 10 March 2009, won 4-0
Barcelona, Champions League semi-final 2nd leg, 7 May 2019, won 4-0

FIVE EUROPEAN CULT HEROES

David Fairclough – for the goal that clinched victory against Saint-Étienne in 1977
Alan Kennedy – for being an unlikely European Cup Final matchwinner in 1981 and 1984
Luis García – for netting vital goals during the run to Istanbul in 2005
Jerzy Dudek – for his goalkeeping heroics that denied AC Milan at the Ataturk in 2005
Divock Origi – for completing the greatest comeback versus Barcelona and then wrapping up number six in Madrid in 2019

DID YOU KNOW?

1. With 13 trophies, Liverpool are out in front as the most successful English club when it comes to continental competition.

2. Bob Paisley was the first manager to win the European Cup/Champions League three times (1977, 1978, 1981) and only Carlo Ancelotti, Zinedine Zidane and Pep Guardiola have since emulated him.

3. It was in the now defunct European Cup Winners' Cup that Liverpool reached a European final for the first time (1966), only to be beaten by Borussia Dortmund in Glasgow.

4. Tommy Smith was the first Liverpool captain to lift a European trophy (1973 UEFA Cup).

5. Liverpool's all-time record victory came in the European Cup Winners' Cup on 17 September 1974, when they defeated Strømsgodset from Norway 11-0 in a 1st round 1st leg tie at Anfield.

6. Five different captains have lifted the European Cup for Liverpool, with Emlyn Hughes the only one to do so twice (1977 and 1978).

7. Phil Neal has won more European Cup winners' medals (four) than any other Liverpool player and scored in two of those finals.

8. Joe Fagan and Rafael Benítez both guided Liverpool to European Cup/Champions League success in their first seasons as manager.

9. Trent Alexander-Arnold is the youngest player to appear in successive Champions League finals (2018 & 2019).

10. In winning a sixth European Cup/Champions League in 2019, Liverpool joined the realms of European royalty, with only two clubs – Real Madrid and AC Milan – having won it more.

11. The fastest hat-trick in Champions League history was scored by Mo Salah when he came off the bench to notch three in just six minutes and 12 seconds away to Rangers in November 2022.

12. Liverpool is the only English club to achieve a 100 percent record in the Champions League group phase, a feat achieved during the 2021/22 season.

all stats correct prior to the 2024/25 season

L.F.C.

CURTIS JONES

17

NATIONALITY:
English

DATE OF BIRTH:
30 January 2001

GAMES: 133

GOALS: 16

ASSISTS: 13

HONOURS:
FA Community Shield (2022),
FA Cup (2022), League Cup
(2022, 2024), Premier League
(2019-20)

L.F.C.

LUIS DÍAZ

7

NATIONALITY:
Colombian

DATE OF BIRTH:
13 January 1997

GAMES: 98

GOALS: 24

ASSISTS: 10

HONOURS:
FA Community Shield (2022),
FA Cup (2022), League Cup
(2022, 2024)

MATT BEARD

Matt Beard's reputation as one of the leading managers in the women's game was further enhanced in 2023/24 when he was named Barclays WSL Manager of the Year for the second time.

Beard, who first won this award in 2013, was recognised by the League Manager's Association for guiding his team to a fourth place finish last term – the club's highest since 2017.

A four-game winning run to end the season – including victories against Manchester United and eventual champions Chelsea – helped seal a spot in the top four.

After finishing seventh the previous campaign Beard said: "We're delighted with the season. These awards are humbling and I'm very, very grateful to everyone that voted. It's not just about me, it's about the team too. They have to go out and perform and the staff work relentlessly behind the scenes to help support everything that we do as well. It's about the collective and that's the staff and the players. Everyone deserves recognition for that."

He added: "I think at the beginning of the season we had a fantastic start by winning at the Emirates [against Arsenal] and I think it gave us that platform to kick on. If you look at May as an example, it was a tough month, we played Bristol City, who at that point weren't relegated and were fighting for every point.

"We then play Chelsea and won 4-3 and then beat Manchester United 1-0 and finish off with a great win at Leicester. If I just look at the consistency of the performance levels and the character within the group in all those games, I think it speaks volumes for the work that has gone on this year.

"I've said this a few times this year, but it's exciting to see where this team can go."

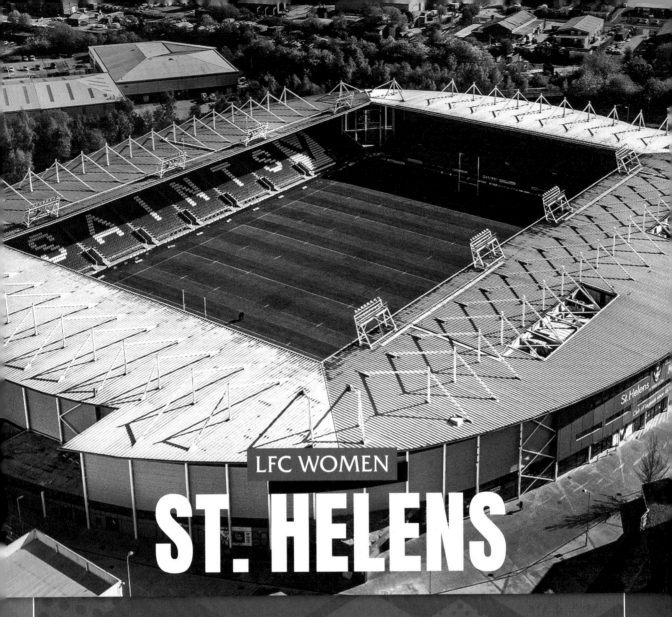

LFC WOMEN
ST. HELENS

The ongoing growth of Liverpool FC Women has not just been confined to actions on the pitch.

Following their move into the club's iconic Melwood training ground last season, an exciting 10-year lease was agreed for the team to play its home games at the impressive St. Helens Stadium from the start of the 2024/25 campaign.

Although the stadium will continue to be the home and property of St. Helens R.F.C, with the rugby league season running from February through to September, LFC Women will have sole occupancy for almost half of the year.

Among the benefits are a brand-new, high-performance Premier League-standard pitch, enhanced and exclusive-use player facilities, and an improved matchday experience for supporters.

The team will also enjoy having their own bespoke dressing room for the first time, and the red stadium will be revamped for home games to make it look and feel part of the LFC family, including the addition of the club crest and other significant branding.

By providing the players, staff and supporters with the best facilities possible, this new deal further demonstrates the club's long-term commitment to the continuing progression of its women's team.

Susan Black, LFC's director of communications and Liverpool FC Women executive director, said: "This is another step forward for our women's first team and we're so excited to relocate to a new long-term home. Our players and incredible supporters were at the forefront of our decision-making process. We are confident St. Helens will be a great matchday home and will look and feel part of the Liverpool family.

"As founding members of the Women's Super League, we want to continue the work we've put in place and continue to progress in the league both on and off the pitch. Our next chapter for our women's first team is about building solid foundation stones and this matchday venue announcement is another positive step forward on our journey."

For all the latest LFC Women ticket information visit https://www.liverpoolfc.com/tickets/tickets-availability-lfc-women

MELWOOD

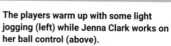

The players warm up with some light jogging (left) while Jenna Clark works on her ball control (above).

Number one Rachel Laws stretches high to tip the ball over the bar.

Olivia Smith practicing her throwing skills.

Zara Shaw and Eva Spencer set out to begin their preparation for the new season.

Marie Höbinger prepares to unleash a shot under the watchful eye of boss Matt Beard.

The LFC Women are put through their paces at the club's iconic training ground in West Derby.

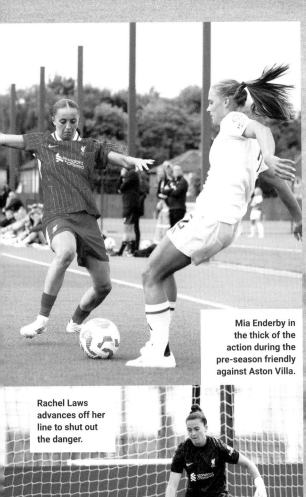

Mia Enderby in the thick of the action during the pre-season friendly against Aston Villa.

Rachel Laws advances off her line to shut out the danger.

The players take to the field at Melwood for their first run-out of summer 2024.

2024/25
FIXTURE TRACKER

BARCLAYS WOMEN'S SUPER LEAGUE

			SCORE
SEPTEMBER			
22	Leicester City	(H)	
29	West Ham United	(A)	
OCTOBER			
6	Tottenham Hotspur	(A)	
13	Manchester City	(H)	
20	Crystal Palace	(H)	
NOVEMBER			
3	Aston Villa	(A)	
10	Chelsea	(H)	
16	Everton	(A)	
DECEMBER			
8	Manchester United	(A)	
15	Arsenal	(H)	
JANUARY			
19	Brighton & Hove Albion	(H)	
26	Leicester City	(A)	
FEBRUARY			
2	West Ham United	(H)	
16	Manchester City	(A)	
MARCH			
2	Crystal Palace	(A)	
16	Manchester United	(H)	
23	Arsenal	(A)	
30	Aston Villa	(H)	
APRIL			
20	Brighton & Hove Albion	(A)	
27	Tottenham Hotspur	(H)	
MAY			
4	Everton	(H)	
TBC	Chelsea	(A)	

DARWIN NÚÑEZ

9

NATIONALITY:
Uruguayan

DATE OF BIRTH:
24 June 1999

GAMES: 96

GOALS: 33

ASSISTS: 17

HONOURS:
FA Community Shield (2022),
League Cup (2024)

L.F.C.

MOHAMED SALAH

11

NATIONALITY:
Egyptian

DATE OF BIRTH:
15 June 1992

GAMES: **349**

GOALS: **211**

ASSISTS: **87**

HONOURS:
FA Community Shield (2022),
FA Cup (2022), League Cup
(2022, 2024), Premier League
(2019-20), Champions
League (2019), UEFA Super
Cup (2019), FIFA Club World
Cup (2019)

EXPERIENCE THE MAGIC OF LFC

Enjoy a whistle-stop tour of the revamped Liverpool FC Museum, Anfield's brand-new immersive experience.

The reimagined space is a fitting tribute to the club's illustrious heritage, with state-of-the-art exhibits showcasing many of the iconic moments, legendary figures and celebrated achievements.

Relaunched in July 2024, following its first major refurbishment in a decade, the integration of cutting-edge technology – including various multimedia installations – has injected fresh life into a story that continues to capture the hearts of our global fanbase.

Discover how the Reds evolved from humble origins to become one of the world's most historic and famous football clubs and learn more about just what it is that makes this club so special.

If you've not yet checked it out, here's a glimpse of what to expect...

Red, White & Silver - in celebration of Liverpool's status as English football's most successful club, all the major trophies have been brought together in one place for the first time ever. A photo opportunity not to be missed!

Danke Jürgen – a special tribute to the glorious managerial reign of Jürgen Klopp that takes a closer look at his most memorable moments and features a groundbreaking hologram of the man himself.

How It All Began – from the 'Team of Macs' in 1892 and the first seeds of success to the unforgettable day at Wembley in 1965 when the FA Cup was won for the first time, retrace the early history of the club.

The Story Of Our Supporters – football is nothing without fans and this section pays homage to the beating heart of our club via various items of match-going memorabilia and a quick dip into the extensive Kop songbook.

European Royalty – be transported back in time to each of the six never-to-be-forgotten occasions when Liverpool have been crowned Kings of Europe and prepare to be dazzled by another glittering collection of silverware.

The Boss – from William Barclay to Arne Slot and Matt Beard, via Bill Shankly, Bob Paisley and many others, find out more about the men who have been entrusted with the ultimate responsibility of being in charge of team affairs at Liverpool.

Legends – when it comes to great players, this club has been blessed and some of the most iconic are remembered through a fascinating collection of boots, medals and match-worn shirts that they've donated.

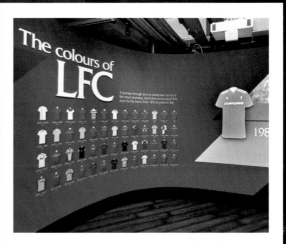

The Colours Of LFC – a journey through time to remember some of the most stunning, distinctive and unusual shirts worn by the team, from 1892 to present day. Everyone has a favourite, but which will be yours?

"The LFC museum is more than just a collection of artefacts; it's a place where we can celebrate the club's heritage and the incredible journey we've shared with our fans. The new space is a modern revamp of our story that remembers our past and looks to our future."

Mike Cox, senior vice-president of museum and tours at Liverpool FC

Did You Know? The LFC Stadium Tour & Museum is one of the city's leading tourist attractions and supports a thriving visitor economy in Liverpool. Last year, just under 400,000 people went behind the scenes at Anfield, and it was also awarded a TripAdvisor Travellers' Choice award, placing it in the top 10 percent of worldwide attractions.

To visit the new and improved LFC museum, which is included in all stadium tours and experiences, book via www.lfctv/tours

LFC CROSSWORD

How well do you know The Reds? Use the clues below to complete the crossword.

Across

2. 2005 Champions League winning captain (6, 7)
4. The _____ Scouser, nickname of Kostas Tsimikas (5)
7. Senegalese striker signed from Southampton and sold to Bayern Munich (5, 4)
8. The team Liverpool defeated to become world champions in 2019 (8)
12. His goal knocked Everton out of the FA Cup in 2020 (6, 5)
14. Word Cup winning Liverpool forward of the 1960s (5, 4)
16.Former Liverpool FC Women's player _____ Bo Kearns (5)
17. Wears the number 66 shirt for Liverpool (5, 9, 6)
18. 1984 treble winning manager (3, 5)
19. Town where the men's first team and academy players train (6)

Down

1. Country where Bill Shankly was born (8)
3. Number of goals scored in the club's all-time record victory (6)
5. City where Liverpool have won two European Cups (4)
6. Former player and manager with a stand named after him at Anfield (3, 5, 8)
9. 2001 Ballon d'Or winner (7, 4)
10. Ben ___, young Scottish winger (4)
11. At the end of a storm there's a... (6, 3)
13. Signed from Porto in 2022 (4, 4)
15. Country captained by Dominik Szoboszlai (7)
16. Jan _____, once scored a hat-trick of penalties in the 1980s (5)

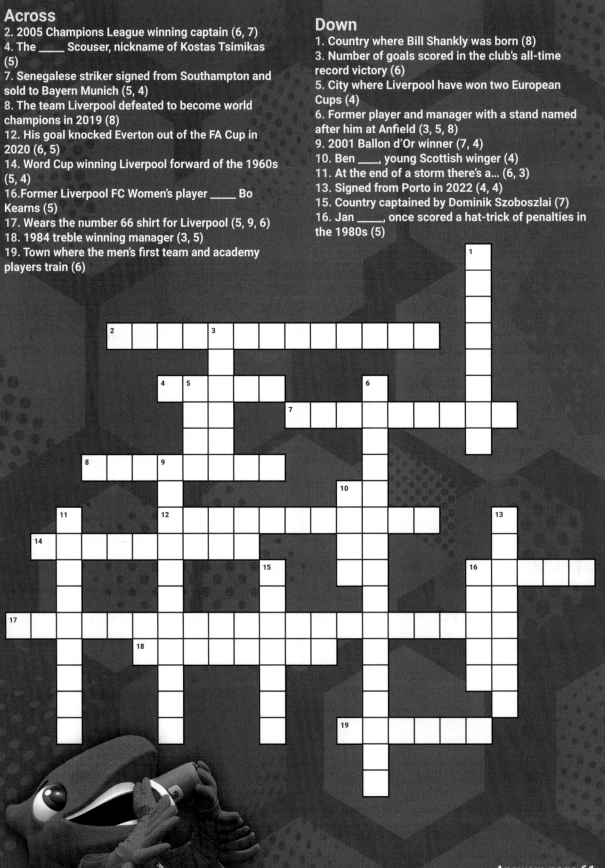

Answers page 61

WHO'S THE BOSS

Search the grid vertically, horizontally and diagonally to uncover the names
of the men who have managed the Reds.

S	U	D	H	N	I	S	Y	E	H	J	Y	P	U
E	Y	D	D	W	O	T	H	S	K	C	I	A	E
C	A	C	F	A	O	S	L	A	R	G	H	I	S
M	K	F	S	T	B	E	R	F	N	O	H	S	N
P	C	O	J	S	W	E	A	E	D	K	I	L	A
T	P	K	F	O	E	G	N	G	T	E	L	E	V
O	V	O	E	N	A	N	S	I	R	T	A	Y	E
L	V	U	L	N	H	O	U	R	T	S	A	Z	C
S	V	Z	Q	K	N	C	Y	O	H	E	G	P	M
H	S	I	L	G	L	A	D	W	S	A	Z	S	K
B	A	R	C	L	A	Y	O	L	P	X	O	O	E
T	A	Y	L	O	R	R	N	E	E	U	Q	C	M
U	Y	W	A	T	T	H	O	U	L	L	I	E	R
S	M	X	Q	H	S	R	E	G	D	O	R	B	K

Barclay	Kay	Fagan	Benitez
McKenna	Welsh	Dalglish	Hodgson
Watson	Taylor	Souness	Rodgers
Ashworth	Shankly	Evans	Klopp
McQueen	Paisley	Houllier	Slot
Patterson			

Answers page 61

L.F.C.

FORWARD

CODY GAKPO

18

NATIONALITY:
Dutch

DATE OF BIRTH:
7 May 1999

GAMES: 79

GOALS: 23

ASSISTS: 8

HONOURS:
League Cup (2024)

L.F.C.

DIOGO JOTA

20

NATIONALITY:
Portuguese

DATE OF BIRTH:
4 December 1996

GAMES: 145

GOALS: 56

ASSISTS: 19

HONOURS:
FA Cup (2022), League Cup
(2022, 2024)

CIAO CHIESA!

A warm welcome to Liverpool for summer signing Federico Chiesa

Profile

Date of Birth:
26 October 1997
Birthplace: **Genoa, Italy**
Height: **5ft 9in**
Position: **Winger/forward**
Joined Liverpool:
29 August 2024
LFC Squad Number:**14**

Previous Clubs
2016-2022 – Fiorentina
2020-2022 – Juventus
 (on loan)
2022-2024 – Juventus

Honours
Coppa Italia (2021 & 2024)
Supercoppa Italia (2021)
UEFA Euro 2020

International Caps for Italy:
51

THE BACK STORY

Chiesa joined Fiorentina's youth set-up, working his way through the ranks towards a senior debut, aged 18, against Juventus in Serie A at the start of the 2016-17 campaign.

He turned out for La Viola 153 times, scoring on 34 occasions, before heading to Juve in October 2020, initially on a two-year loan deal that became permanent in May 2022.

Towards the end of a brilliant first season in Turin, Chiesa scored the winner in the 2021 Coppa Italia final versus Atalanta.

He would suffer an anterior cruciate ligament injury halfway through the following campaign that kept him sidelined for nearly 10 months.

Getting back on track after the setback, Chiesa's final season at Juve would be his best there in terms of the number of league appearances (33). He netted 10 goals from his 37 outings in all competitions and collected a second Coppa Italia winner's medal.

At international level, the attacker was part of Italy's winning Euro 2020 side, turning out in all seven games, scoring twice and earning himself a place in UEFA's official Team of the Tournament line-up. More recently, Chiesa featured four times for the Azzurri at Euro 2024.

Federico, how does it feel to be a Liverpool player?
"I'm so happy to be a Liverpool player. When Richard Hughes called me and he said, 'Do you want to join Liverpool?' – and the coach called me – I said yes immediately because I know the history of this club, I know what it represents to the fans."

Was it an easy decision to make?
"It was. It was for a lot of reasons because I felt immediately that the people I talked to put a lot of faith and trust in me, and that's what I wanted. So it's really great to be here, it's a dream come true for me to play for Liverpool and to play in the Premier League, which is the best Championship in the world."

What were your first impressions of the club?
"The people here are amazing and I felt great empathy. When I was about to land [in] the aeroplane, I saw Anfield and as soon as I saw Anfield I said to my wife, 'Put the song on' – You'll Never Walk Alone – because I wanted to imagine myself playing there and hearing the chant of the fans.'"

What kind of things did Arne Slot say to you about coming to Liverpool?
"He just told me about his football style, what he wants from me, what he wants from the team. I said to him that I'm coming to help the team and to win trophies, which is the most important thing [and] it's what the Liverpool fans want the most."

Obviously you join a squad with a lot of good attacking options...
"I mean, in Liverpool there is a lot of competition in every role because it's a big club, it's a top club, one of the best in the world. So I know that I was coming here with a lot of competition in my role too because in front of me there are players like [Mohamed] Salah, Luis Díaz, Cody Gakpo, [Diogo] Jota, [Darwin] Núñez. I know what they are capable of, but I know what I am capable of too. So, I'm here to give my best and to give my best to the fans too."

You took the number 14 jersey, is that a number that has any significance to you?
"Yeah, it is actually. It's the number I've been wearing with the national team but it was an easy pick because Liverpool sent me a video and at the end of this video – which was showing my career [and] the goals I scored with Fiorentina and Juventus – it was me with the No.14 shirt on so I said, 'Ah, it was destined to be!', so I chose the No.14."

Italian Reds

Federico Chiesa becomes the seventh player born in Italy to represent Liverpool, following in the footsteps of...
• Daniele Padelli
• Andrea Dossena
• Alberto Aquilani
• Fabio Borini
• Mario Balotelli
• Thiago Alcântara

Did You Know?

Federico's father Enrico played and scored at Anfield for Italy against Czech Republic in Euro 96.

CAOIMHÍN KELLEHER

62

NATIONALITY:
Irish

DATE OF BIRTH:
23 November 1998

GAMES: 47

GOALS: 0

ASSISTS: 0

HONOURS:
Honours: FA Cup (2022),
League Cup (2022, 2024),
Premier League (2019-20),
Champions League (2019),
UEFA Super Cup (2019)

JARELL QUANSAH

DEFENDER

78

NATIONALITY:
English

DATE OF BIRTH:
29 January 2003

GAMES: 33

GOALS: 3

ASSISTS: 3

HONOURS:
League Cup (2024)

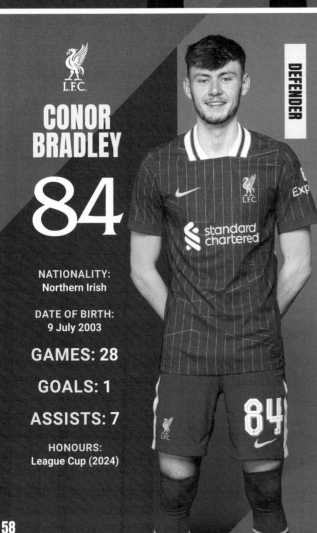

CONOR BRADLEY

DEFENDER

84

NATIONALITY:
Northern Irish

DATE OF BIRTH:
9 July 2003

GAMES: 28

GOALS: 1

ASSISTS: 7

HONOURS:
League Cup (2024)

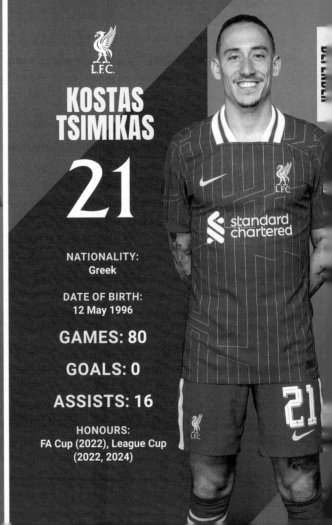

KOSTAS TSIMIKAS

DEFENDER

21

NATIONALITY:
Greek

DATE OF BIRTH:
12 May 1996

GAMES: 80

GOALS: 0

ASSISTS: 16

HONOURS:
FA Cup (2022), League Cup
(2022, 2024)

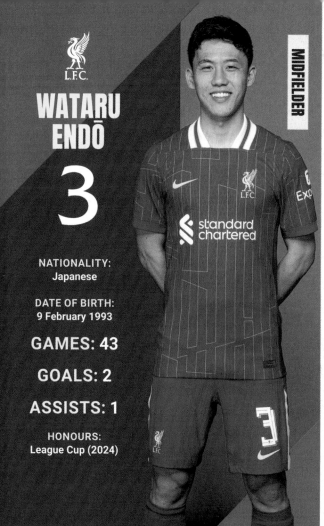

WATARU ENDŌ

MIDFIELDER

3

NATIONALITY:
Japanese

DATE OF BIRTH:
9 February 1993

GAMES: 43

GOALS: 2

ASSISTS: 1

HONOURS:
League Cup (2024)

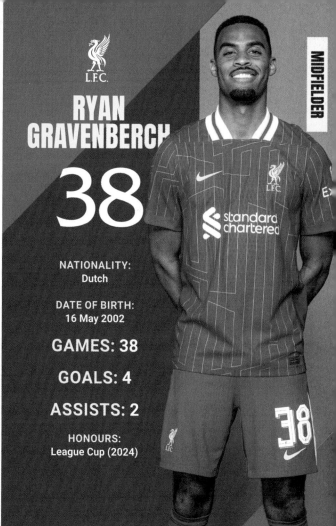

RYAN GRAVENBERCH

MIDFIELDER

38

NATIONALITY:
Dutch

DATE OF BIRTH:
16 May 2002

GAMES: 38

GOALS: 4

ASSISTS: 2

HONOURS:
League Cup (2024)

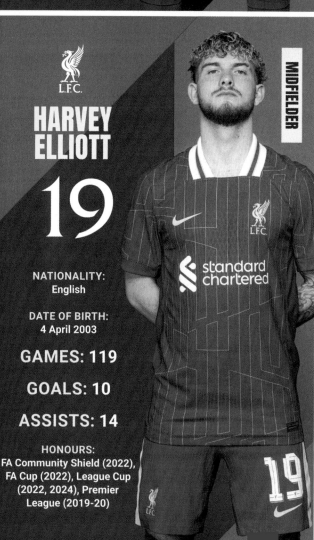

HARVEY ELLIOTT

MIDFIELDER

19

NATIONALITY:
English

DATE OF BIRTH:
4 April 2003

GAMES: 119

GOALS: 10

ASSISTS: 14

HONOURS:
FA Community Shield (2022),
FA Cup (2022), League Cup
(2022, 2024), Premier
League (2019-20)

2024/25 FIXTURE TRACKER

PREMIER LEAGUE

AUGUST — SCORE

17	Ipswich Town	(A)
25	Brentford	(H)
31	Manchester United	(A)

SEPTEMBER

14	Nottingham Forest	(H)
21	Bournemouth	(H)
28	Wolverhampton Wanderers	(A)

OCTOBER

5	Crystal Palace	(A)
19	Chelsea	(H)
26	Arsenal	(A)

NOVEMBER

2	Brighton & Hove Albion	(H)
9	Aston Villa	(H)
23	Southampton	(A)
30	Manchester City	(H)

DECEMBER

4	Newcastle United	(A)
7	Everton	(A)
14	Fulham	(H)
21	Tottenham Hotspur	(A)
26	Leicester City	(H)
29	West Ham United	(A)

JANUARY

4	Manchester United	(H)
14	Nottingham Forest	(A)
18	Brentford	(A)
25	Ipswich Town	(H)

FEBRUARY

1	Bournemouth	(A)
15	Wolverhampton Wanderers	(H)
22	Manchester City	(A)
26	Newcastle United	(H)

MARCH

8	Southampton	(H)
15	Aston Villa	(A)

APRIL

2	Everton	(H)
5	Fulham	(A)
12	West Ham United	(H)
19	Leicester City	(A)
26	Tottenham Hotspur	(H)

MAY

3	Chelsea	(A)
10	Arsenal	(H)
18	Brighton & Hove Albion	(A)
25	Crystal Palace	(H)

CHAMPIONS LEAGUE

SEPTEMBER — vs & SCORE

17	AC Milan (A)

OCTOBER

2	Bologna (H)
23	RB Leipzig (A)

NOVEMBER

5	Bayer Leverkusen (H)
27	Real Madrid (H)

DECEMBER

10	Girona (A)

JANUARY

21	Lille (H)
29	PSV Eindhoven (A)

FEBRUARY

11/12	Knockout round play-off 1st leg
18/19	Knockout round play-off 2nd leg

MARCH

4/5	Round of 16 1st leg
11/12	Round of 16 2nd leg

APRIL

8/9	Quarter-final 1st leg
15/16	Quarter-final 2nd leg
29/30	Semi-final 1st leg

MAY

6/7	Semi-final 2nd leg
31	FINAL (Munich)

FA CUP

		vs & SCORE
January 1	3rd round	
February 8	4th round	
March 1	5th round	
March 29	Quarter-final	
April 26	Semi-final	
May 17	FINAL (WEMBLEY)	

LEAGUE CUP

		vs & SCORE
September 25	3rd round	
October 30	4th round	
December 18	5th round	
January 8	Semi-final 1st leg	
February 5	Semi-final 2nd leg	
March 16	FINAL (WEMBLEY)	

INTERNATIONAL BREAKS
September 7, October 12 , November 16 , March 22

All fixtures subject to change

ANSWERS

Page 28-29: The Big Liverpool FC Quiz

General Knowledge
1. Jarell Quansah
2. Feyenoord
3. Watford
4. Jordan Henderson
5. Bournemouth
6. Northern Ireland
7. The Hawthorns
8. Harvey Elliott
9. June
10. Cody Gakpo
11. FA Cup
12. Chelsea
13. Roberto Firmino
14. Twice
15. Spain

Retro Reds
1. Ajax
2. Ian Callaghan
3. Four
4. Gerard Houllier
5. Ian Rush

Which Liverpool player am I?
1. Ryan Gravenberch
2. Darwin Núñez
3. Joe Gomez
4. Virgil van Dijk
5. Mohamed Salah

Missing Men
Luis Díaz & Jarell Quansah

Up For The Cup
FA Cup - 1965
UEFA Cup - 1973
European Cup - 1977
League Cup - 1981
FIFA Club World Cup - 2019

Transfer Window
1. Andy Robertson
2. Mohamed Salah
3. Alexis Mac Allister
4. Diogo Jota
5. Wataru Endō

Page 35: Spot the Difference

Page 52: Crossword

Across / Down answers shown in grid:
SCOTLAND, STEVENGERRARD, GREEK, SADIOMANE, FLAMENGO, CURTISJONES, ROGERHUNT, MISSY, TRENTALEXANDERARNOLD, JOEFAGAN, KIRKBY, LUISDIAZ

Page 53: Wordsearch

S	U	D	H	N	I	S	Y	E	H	J	Y	P	U
E	Y	D	D	W	O	T	H	S	K	C	I	A	E
C	A	C	F	A	O	S	L	A	R	G	H	I	S
M	K	F	S	T	B	E	R	F	N	O	H	S	N
P	C	O	J	S	W	E	A	E	D	K	I	L	A
T	P	K	F	O	E	G	N	G	T	E	L	E	V
O	V	O	E	N	A	N	S	I	R	T	A	Y	E
L	V	U	L	N	H	O	U	R	T	S	A	Z	C
S	V	Z	Q	K	N	C	Y	O	H	E	G	P	M
H	S	I	L	G	L	A	D	W	S	A	Z	S	K
B	A	R	C	L	A	Y	O	L	P	X	O	O	E
T	A	Y	L	O	R	R	N	E	E	U	Q	C	M
U	Y	W	A	T	T	H	O	U	L	L	I	E	R
S	M	X	Q	H	S	R	E	G	D	O	R	B	K

SPOT THE PLAYERS

Can you spot the five LFC players hiding in the crowd at Anfield?

standard chartered